THE INTERNET

KERRY COCHRANE

A First Book

FRANKLIN WATTS
A Division of Grolier Publishing
New York   London   Hong Kong   Sydney
Danbury, Connecticut

Cover art by Roman Luba
Interior book design by Carole Desnoes

Photographs copyright ©: Bolt Beranek & Newman Inc.: p.6; Photo Researchers: p. 10 (Christian Grzimek/OKAPIA).

Note on Internet addresses: The periods and commas following some of the Internet addresses in this book are never part of the addresses themselves and appear only for grammatical reasons.

Prodigy, America Online, and Spry are trademarks of their respective companies.

Library of Congress Cataloging-in-Publication Data

Cochrane, Kerry.
    The Internet / Kerry Cochrane.
        p. cm. — (A First book)
    Includes bibliographical references and index.
    Summary: An introduction to the Internet, a worldwide network of computers that communicate with each other, and its many uses.
    ISBN 0-531-20200-3
    1. Internet (Computer network)—Juvenile literature.
[1. Internet (Computer network) 2. Computers.] I. Title. II. Series.
TK5105.875.I57C62 1995   95-23325
004.6'7—dc20   CIP AC

Contents

TITLE

Introduction

Who hasn't heard about the Internet? It's mentioned on television, in the magazines, and on the radio. Everyone's talking about it, and everyone wants to get connected to it. But what is the Internet? It isn't a place or an organization. No one person or company or country runs it, and no one owns it. The Internet is a worldwide network of computers that communicate with each other. Although the Internet works like one seamless network, it is really made up of many smaller networks linking thousands of different computers. These networks connect computers run by government agencies, small companies, huge corporations, public schools, public libraries, universities, and not-for-profit organizations. This book will introduce you to the Internet, how it works, and what you can do on it.

In the late 1960s, The United States Department of Defense began to develop a computer network, called the Advanced Research Projects Agency network (ARPAnet), that would not be vulnerable to bomb attacks. If the army built a network with many machines connected to a powerful central computer, one bomb dropped on the central computer could cripple the entire network. The Department of Defense needed to set up a web of computers that could communicate easily with each other even if a few of the computers were disabled.

At that time, most computer centers operated independently. There was no *standard* for networking software, so programmers had to write new computer programs for one machine to work with another one. The challenge for ARPAnet was to design a system that would let computers all over the country work together without needing special programming. This would make it harder to disrupt communication in case of war, because any one computer could be destroyed without affecting the network as a whole. ARPAnet originally wired together four sites in

► Information on the history of the Internet is available on-line from the Charles Babbage Institute of the University of Minnesota. Their World Wide Web address is **http://fs1.itdean.umn. edu/cbi/cbihome.html.**

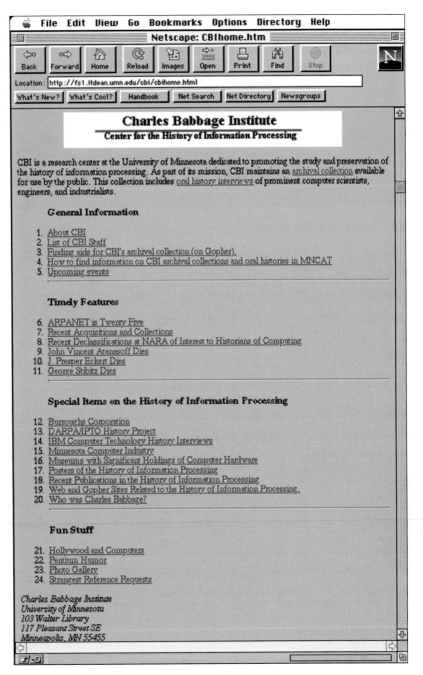

◄ The IMP Development Group was a key team of developers for the ARPAnet project. Pictured here around 1970 are (left to right) Truett Thach (seated), Bill Bartell, Dave Walden, Jim Geisman, Bob Kahn, Frank Heart, Ben Barker, Martin Thrope, Will Crowther, and Severo Ornstein.

the western United States. This experimental network has since evolved into the vast worldwide network called the Internet.

The most important resource on the Internet is the people connected to it: students, researchers, business people, librarians, and government officials. People can connect to the Internet from a personal computer at home, a *workstation* in their office, a computer network in school, or public workstations in their library. Students use the Internet to share projects with schools in other countries. Researchers collaborate with each other on the Internet without ever meeting face to face. People of all ages and nationalities use the Internet to discuss recreational interests. The White House has an Internet mailbox to receive messages from the public. Businesses offer their products for sale on-line through an Internet mall. During the downfall of the Soviet Union, when it was almost impossible for the Russian people to communicate outside their country, the Internet provided the most reliable means of sending messages back and forth. The Internet has grown far beyond its original purpose of sending military information. Its uses are now as varied as its users.

CHAPTER

TITLE

How the Internet Works

The central problem in designing the Internet was finding a way for different kinds of computers all over the country to talk to one another. ARPA solved this problem with Internet protocols. Protocols are sets of rules that standardize how something is done, so that everyone knows what to expect. For example, think of any game you've played and the rules that went with that game. The rules of the game tell you how many players you can have, what order you play in, what's allowed and what's not allowed, and how to keep score. Once you know the rules, you can play with people very different from you. Internet protocols are like game rules: they set up standard procedures for computers to follow so that they can communicate with each other.

The Internet is often compared to the postal service. They both seem to work like one big organization, but are actually made up of smaller parts that work together. There are local post offices in small towns, regional postal systems in big cities, and

Protocols allow post offices around the world to work together. As a result, postal workers can use many different methods to carry mail from New York City to this remote post box in Ecuador. Internet protocols serve a similar purpose.

national postal services for countries. They all use different machinery to handle the mail, and different equipment to deliver it, from bicycles to trucks to airplanes. Postal workers all over the world speak hundreds of different languages. But they all manage to work together because of certain rules, or protocols. Postal protocols say that mail must be in envelopes or packages, there must be postage, and every piece of mail must have an address. As long as you know these rules, you can send mail to anyone in the world.

The Internet works in a similar way. As long as everyone

knows the protocols, information can travel easily between machines and the people using them worldwide. The basic group of protocols that governs the Internet is the TCP/IP set of protocols. This stands for Transmission Control Protocol (TCP) and Internet Protocol (IP). Internet Protocol says that every computer connected to the Internet must have a unique address. These addresses consist of four sets of numbers separated by periods. For example, the IP address for one of the computers at the University of Illinois at Urbana-Champaign is **128.174.5.49**. Once you have the IP address of a computer, you know where to send messages or other information. Transmission Control Protocol manages the information you send out by computer. TCP breaks each message into manageable chunks and numbers each chunk in order. Then the numbered groups of information are marked with the IP address of the other computer and are sent out to it. When they arrive on the other end, TCP software checks to see that all the pieces are there and puts them back in order, ready for use.

When you drop a letter into a mailbox, it gets collected and sorted with hundreds of other pieces of mail. Your local post office sorts and routes the mail according to its destination and then sends it on to the next post office. Information is sorted and routed on the Internet in the same way. Computers on the Internet called routers, or packet switchers, read the IP addresses on each packet of information, and direct the packets to their destination. The information can be sent from one computer to another on phone lines, by satellite networks, on fiber-optic cables, or even through radio transmissions.

IP addresses are made up of numbers, which can be hard to remember and use. So computers usually have alphabetical addresses as well. Like IP addresses, these alphabetical addresses have several parts separated by periods, although they may have fewer or more than four parts. So a computer at the University of Iowa with the IP address **128.255.40.201** also has the alphabetical address **panda.uiowa.edu**, which is easier to remember. The first part of this address, **panda**, is the name of the *host* computer. The rest of this address, **uiowa.edu**, is called a domain name, because each part of the name refers to a domain. Each domain gives information about the Internet site, such as where it's located, who's responsible for the computer, and what kind of institution it's connected to. Moving from right to left, the domains give more specific information about the location of the host computer. In the domain name **uiowa.edu**, for example, the domain **edu** tells you that the host computer is run by an educational institution, because **edu** is the domain attached to all United States educational sites. The domain **uiowa** stands for the University of Iowa, which is the specific educational institution where the host computer named panda is located.

In the United States, there are six domains that are used at the end of domain names, and each one refers to the type of site that's running the computer.

domain	definition	example
com	companies or commercial sites	apple.com (Apple corporation)
edu	educational sites	yale.edu (Yale University)
gov	U.S. government sites	nasa.gov (NASA)
mil	U.S. military sites	ddn.mil (Defense Department Network)
net	network sites	digex.net (Digex Internet service)
org	private organizations	carl.org (Colorado Alliance of Research Libraries)

Countries outside the United States do not use these domains. Instead, they have two-letter country domains at the end of their names, such as **nz** for New Zealand, **br** for Brazil, or **ca** for Canada.

Every person with an Internet *account* has a personal address, too. Individual Internet addresses are made up of a unique *user ID* (sometimes called a user name) for each person, which is attached to an alphabetical address by an "at" symbol (@). User IDs are usually taken from your name. My full Internet address is **kcochra@orion.it.luc.edu**. Reading this address from left to right, you see that my user ID is **kcochra** (from Kerry Cochrane), and I'm at the address **orion.it.luc.edu**. **Orion** is the name of the host machine running this account. The office of Information Technologies runs the computer named orion, so the first domain is called **it**. Information Technologies is an office of Loyola University Chicago, so the next domain is **luc**. Because this is an educational institution, the final domain is **edu**. The President of the United States even has an Internet address at the White House: **president@whitehouse.gov**. Although they may seem complicated at first, Internet addresses make sense when you know how they work.

A few years ago the Internet was not available to the general public. Most people with Internet accounts got them through universities or companies where they were students or employees. As interest in the Internet has grown, however, ways to connect have increased, and they are improving all the time. One of the fastest-growing groups of Internet users is students and teachers in kindergarten through 12th grade. Schools around the world are getting access to the Internet so children can benefit from the immense resources available on-line.

There are several ways for schools to connect to the Internet. Many states or regions have developed their own networks to link

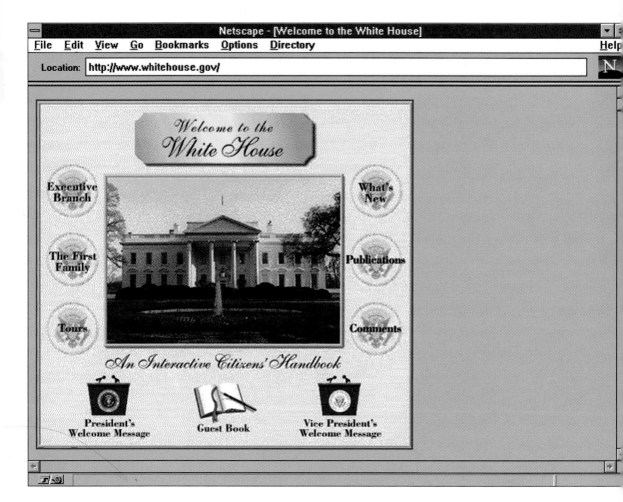

In addition to having an E-mail address, the president also has a Web page at the White House. This site offers lots of information about the White House including an audible welcome message from the president and virtual tours. This site can be reached at **http://www.whitehouse.gov.**

schools together and get them on-line. Some universities and colleges provide guest accounts for local schools. Also, companies called Internet providers have begun to market Internet accounts to schools, companies, and private individuals. Your school may already be connected to the Internet, or someone in your family may have an account at work or at home.

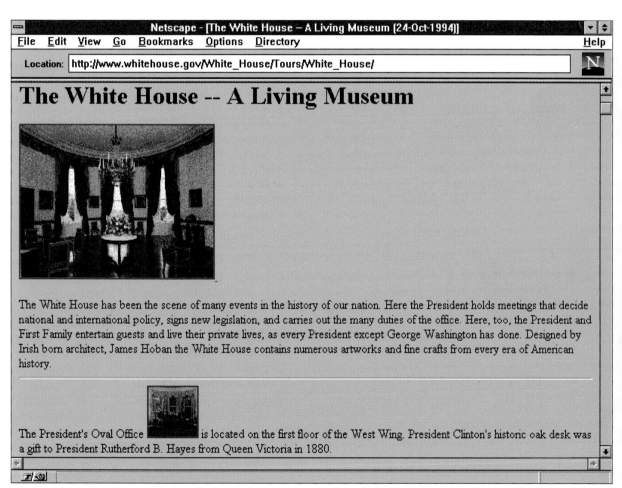

The White House has been the scene of many events in the history of our nation. Here the President holds meetings that decide national and international policy, signs new legislation, and carries out the many duties of the office. Here, too, the President and First Family entertain guests and live their private lives, as every President except George Washington has done. Designed by Irish born architect, James Hoban the White House contains numerous artworks and fine crafts from every era of American history.

The President's Oval Office is located on the first floor of the West Wing. President Clinton's historic oak desk was a gift to President Rutherford B. Hayes from Queen Victoria in 1880.

It is important to understand the many different kinds of connections to the Internet, especially if you want to get your own account. Different kinds of connections have very different capabilities. The fastest and most versatile type of connection uses a dedicated high speed cable, usually called a line, that runs directly between your computer and the Internet. With this type of connection, information can travel between your computer and the rest of the Internet 24 hours a day, as long as your computer is turned on. Your machine has a permanent IP address, and can run any compatible software that conforms to the TCP/IP set of protocols. This kind of connection is very expensive, so it is only common at colleges, schools, and corporations, including commercial Internet providers. However, even if your computer isn't connected this way, it likely communicates with several computers that are. For example, mail *servers*, the computers that receive, send, and sort mail, must be able to receive messages 24 hours a day, so they usually are connected in this manner.

As long as mail servers hold messages for you until you are ready to log in, however, there is no reason why the average home user needs a full time connection. There are many varieties of these temporary connections. To use these connections, your computer must be connected to a *modem*, which allows data to be sent over phone lines. The speed at which this data is sent depends on the modem and the type of connection. Information travels between your computer and the rest of the Internet only while you are logged on. When you log off, your computer disconnects, freeing the phone line.

The most limited, and usually cheapest kind of temporary connection is a dial-up shell account. With this type of connection, your computer does not have its own IP address; it is connected to a *remote* computer which is itself connected to the Internet. Consequently, it is a particularly indirect and often slow

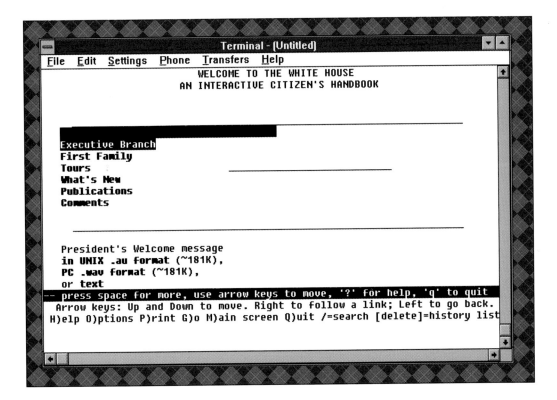

WELCOME TO THE WHITE HOUSE
AN INTERACTIVE CITIZEN'S HANDBOOK

Executive Branch
First Family
Tours
What's New
Publications
Comments

President's Welcome message
in UNIX .au format (~181K),
PC .wav format (~181K),
or text
-- press space for more, use arrow keys to move, '?' for help, 'q' to quit
 Arrow keys: Up and Down to move. Right to follow a link; Left to go back.
H)elp O)ptions P)rint G)o M)ain screen Q)uit /=search [delete]=history list

Character-based Internet programs cannot show pictures, so they are not as friendly as their graphical counterparts. Compare the White House welcome page as displayed here by Lynx, a character-based Web browser, to the same page displayed by Netscape, a graphical browser, on page 14.

way to connect. All the programs that you use to check mail, read news, and *download* files actually reside on the hard disk of the remote computer that you are logged on to. You must use these programs, so the selection is very limited. Also, this connection uses a character-based *terminal* program to display information on your computer screen. This means that your screen can only

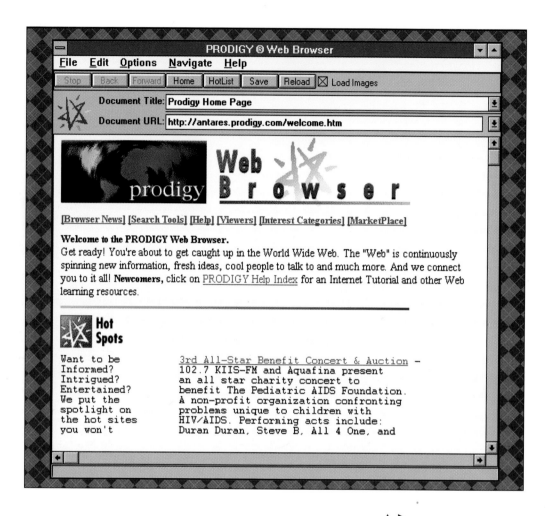

PRODIGY ® Web Browser

File   Edit   Options   Navigate   Help

Stop   Back   Forward   Home   HotList   Save   Reload   ☒ Load Images

Document Title: Prodigy Home Page

Document URL: http://antares.prodigy.com/welcome.htm

prodigy **Web Browser**

[Browser News] [Search Tools] [Help] [Viewers] [Interest Categories] [MarketPlace]

Welcome to the PRODIGY Web Browser.

Get ready! You're about to get caught up in the World Wide Web. The "Web" is continuously spinning new information, fresh ideas, cool people to talk to and much more. And we connect you to it all! **Newcomers,** click on PRODIGY Help Index for an Internet Tutorial and other Web learning resources.

Hot Spots

Want to be Informed? Intrigued? Entertained? We put the spotlight on the hot sites you won't

3rd All-Star Benefit Concert & Auction – 102.7 KIIS-FM and Aquafina present an all star charity concert to benefit The Pediatric AIDS Foundation. A non-profit organization confronting problems unique to children with HIV/AIDS. Performing acts include: Duran Duran, Steve B, All 4 One, and

▲►
Prodigy and America Online offer many of the advantages of SLIP/PPP accounts, though you must use the software they provide. As these examples show, their programs are highly graphical.

show letters, numbers, and other assorted symbols. Consequently, using a graphical program that displays pictures and icons that can be selected with a mouse is impossible. Despite its limitations, a dial-up shell account can be a very useful and economical connection for a person who uses only E-mail or doesn't mind the relative unfriendliness of character-based programs.

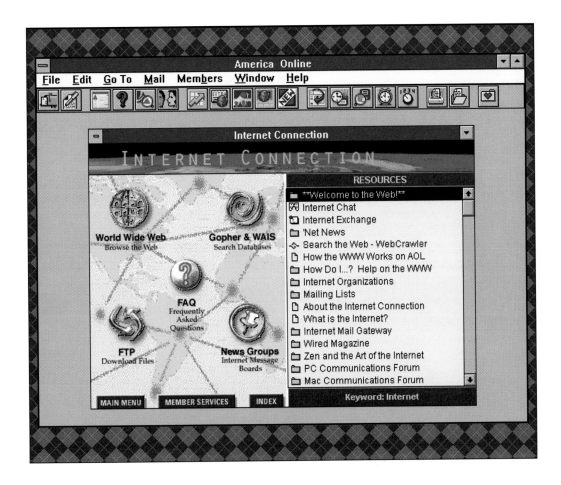

For a long time, the dial-up shell account was the only widely available alternative to a direct connection. However, there are now some other very attractive options. Serial Line Internet Protocol (SLIP) and Point to Point Protocol (PPP) connections both offer many of the advantages of a permanent connection at a much lower price. Like a dial-up shell account, these connections use phone lines to send data and are only active while you are logged on to your account. Unlike a dial-up shell connection, however, computers connected with SLIP and PPP accounts behave as though they are directly connected to the Internet while the connection is open. This means that the connected computer has an IP address and can run the large selection of TCP/IP-compliant software available, so it is nearly as versatile as a computer with a permanent connection. Of course, SLIP and PPP connections are somewhat slower than permanent line connections, depending on the speed of the modem.

Some temporary connections are hybrids of shell and SLIP/PPP connections. They use non-standard protocols that prohibit the use of independent TCP/IP software. People with these accounts must use the software furnished by their Internet providers. Many of these providers, however, incorporate the benefits of TCP/IP software into their own software. Consequently, they may provide their users with powerful graphical programs for using gopher and the World Wide Web. Because the different Internet functions are often integrated in this type of software, newcomers to the Internet may find this option less overwhelming. Many popular on-line services, such as America Online, Prodigy, and The Pipeline fall into this category. Once you get a User ID and you know your Internet address, you're ready to start exploring the Internet!

CHAPTER

1 2 3 4

TITLE

Major Internet Functions

Electronic Mail

Once you have an Internet address, you can send and receive electronic mail. E-mail is the system that lets you send messages from your Internet address to someone else's. You can send E-mail messages to one person or to several people at once. Even if you live in a small and isolated town, electronic mail allows you to communicate instantly with kids across the state or around the world.

E-mail programs allow you to compose and send mail, check for new messages you have received, and read these messages. They also allow you to store these messages on your hard drive. To send someone E-mail, you must know their personal address, such as **kcochra@orion.it.luc.edu**. When composing messages, the E-mail program asks for the address, and provides a space for you to write a short subject line. When you are through writing a message, you tell the E-mail program to send

21

it. It usually only takes a few minutes for the message to get to its destination, even if it is thousands of miles away.

Mailing Lists and Newsgroups

People quickly discovered that they could use E-mail to talk with others about common interests, and they set up two ways to do this: mailing lists (also called list servers) and newsgroups. There are thousands of these discussion systems available, covering every conceivable recreational or academic topic. Both mailing lists and newsgroups bring people together on-line, but they have some important differences.

Mailing lists work by subscription, like magazines: you send your Internet address to the address of the mailing list and ask to subscribe. There are many lists for and about children on the Internet. Among the oldest are the four **KIDCAFE** mailing lists run by the KIDLINK society in Norway. The purpose of these lists is to provide global dialogue for kids between the ages of ten and fourteen. The four lists are:

KIDCAFE-INDIVIDUAL for individual kids to join and find "keypals" around the world

KIDCAFE-SCHOOL for school groups to send mail to other schools

▶

Many Internet programs are available in versions for both Microsoft Windows and the Macintosh. This is the case for this E-mail program called Eudora. The top screen is of a message received by the Windows version. In the bottom screen, the correspondent is composing a reply using the Macintosh version. The text preceded by greater-than signs is quoted from the original message.

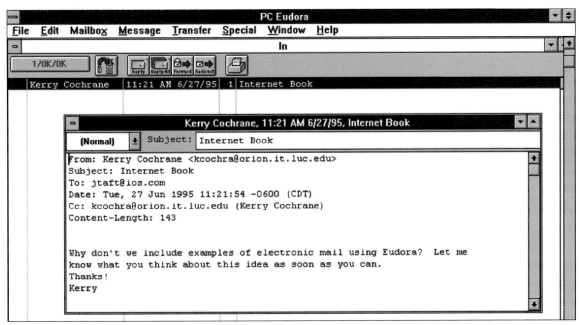

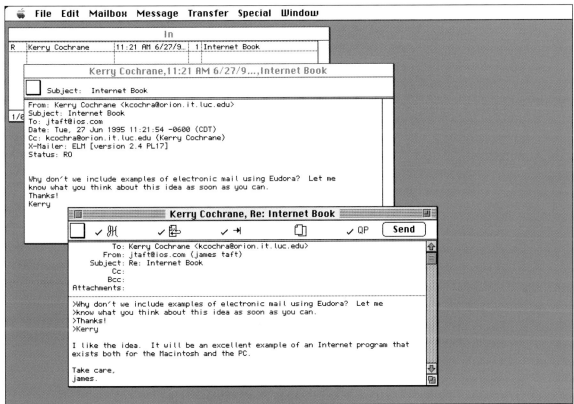

KIDCAFE-TOPIC	for open discussion on topics of interest
KIDCAFE-QUERY	for young researchers to ask questions or take surveys

Most list servers have one address for sending subscription requests and another for sending notes, called posts, to other subscribers. To subscribe to a **KIDCAFE** mailing list, send an electronic mail message to the subscription address for the four lists, **listserv@vm1.nodak.edu**. Your subscription message contains the word **SUBSCRIBE**, or the abbreviation **SUB**, followed by the name of the specific list you wish to join and your own name. For example, Eleanor Roosevelt would subscribe to the **KIDCAFE-INDIVIDUAL** list by sending a message containing the words: **SUB KIDCAFE-INDIVIDUAL Eleanor Roosevelt**. After you send a message like this one, your name and Internet address are added to the list of subscribers. All discussion on the list will come right to your electronic mailbox. When you're ready to send posts to this list, send them to the post address, which is **KIDCAFE-INDIVIDUAL@ vm1.nodak.edu**. Every note you send to this address will go to all the other subscribers.

Newsgroups do not work by subscription, however. They are more like bulletin board systems that you can read whenever you want, browsing until you find something of interest.

▶

Shown here are several newsreaders. They are (top to bottom) AIR News for the PC by Spry, News-Watcher for the Macintosh, and tin, a character-based newsreader. With these readers, you can select newsgroups, browse posts to the groups, read the posts, and compose your own responses.

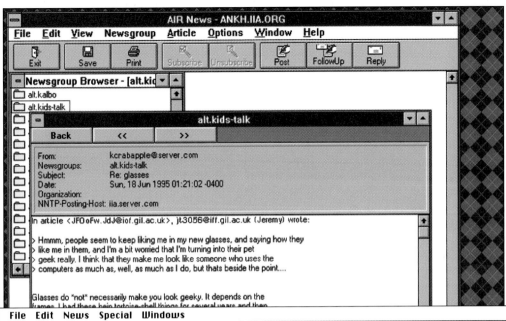

AIR News - ANKH.IIA.ORG

File Edit View Newsgroup Article Options Window Help

Exit   Save   Print   Subscribe Unsubscribe Post FollowUp Reply

Newsgroup Browser - [alt.kid ▼

alt.kalbo
alt.kids-talk

alt.kids-talk

Back   <<   >>

From: kcrabapple@server.com
Newsgroups: alt.kids-talk
Subject: Re: glasses
Date: Sun, 18 Jun 1995 01:21:02 -0400
Organization:
NNTP-Posting-Host: iia.server.com

In article <JFOoFw.JdJ@iof.gil.ac.uk>, jt3056@iff.gil.ac.uk (Jeremy) wrote:

> Hmmm, people seem to keep liking me in my new glasses, and saying how they
> like me in them, and I'm a bit worried that I'm turning into their pet
> geek really. I think that they make me look like someone who uses the
> computers as much as, well, as much as I do, but thats beside the point....

Glasses do "not" necessarily make you look geeky. It depends on the
frames. I had these bein tortoise-shell things for several years and then

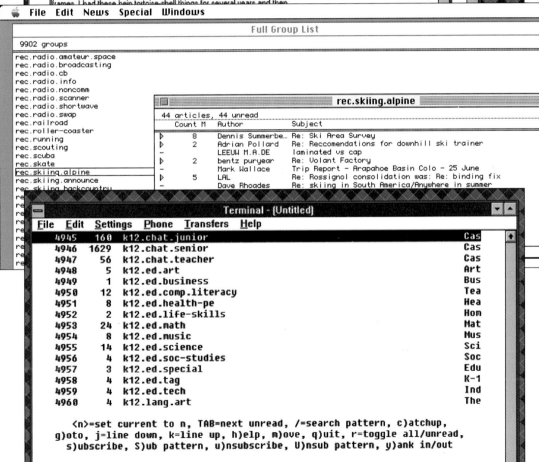

File Edit News Special Windows

Full Group List

9902 groups

rec.radio.amateur.space
rec.radio.broadcasting
rec.radio.cb
rec.radio.info
rec.radio.noncomm
rec.radio.scanner
rec.radio.shortwave
rec.radio.swap
rec.railroad
rec.roller-coaster
rec.running
rec.scouting
rec.scuba
rec.skate
rec.skiing.alpine
rec.skiing.announce
rec.skiing.backcountry

rec.skiing.alpine

44 articles, 44 unread
        Count M Author   Subject
▷   8   Dennis Summerbe… Re: Ski Area Survey
▷   2   Adrian Pollard   Re: Reccomendations for downhill ski trainer
-                LEEUW M.A.DE   laminated vs cap
▷   2   bentz puryear   Re: Volant Factory
-                Mark Wallace   Trip Report - Arapahoe Basin Colo - 25 June
▷   5   LAL   Re: Rossignol consolidation was: Re: binding fix
-                Dave Rhoades   Re: skiing in South America/Anywhere in summer

Terminal - (Untitled)

File Edit Settings Phone Transfers Help

    4945   160   k12.chat.junior   Cas
    4946   1629   k12.chat.senior   Cas
    4947   56   k12.chat.teacher   Cas
    4948   5   k12.ed.art   Art
    4949   1   k12.ed.business   Bus
    4950   12   k12.ed.comp.literacy   Tea
    4951   8   k12.ed.health-pe   Hea
    4952   2   k12.ed.life-skills   Hom
    4953   24   k12.ed.math   Mat
    4954   8   k12.ed.music   Mus
    4955   14   k12.ed.science   Sci
    4956   4   k12.ed.soc-studies   Soc
    4957   3   k12.ed.special   Edu
    4958   4   k12.ed.tag   K-1
    4959   4   k12.ed.tech   Ind
    4960   4   k12.lang.art   The

    <n>=set current to n, TAB=next unread, /=search pattern, c)atchup,
  g)oto, j=line down, k=line up, h)elp, m)ove, q)uit, r=toggle all/unread,
   s)ubscribe, S)ub pattern, u)nsubscribe, U)nsub pattern, y)ank in/out

Instead of having all mail from a group come to you, you scan the subjects of each post to a newsgroup and read only those messages that catch your eye. The difference between subscribing to mailing lists and reading newsgroups is like the difference between subscribing to magazines and going to the library. Imagine if you subscribed to every magazine that might have an interesting article in it. Pretty soon magazines would start filling up your mailbox at home, you'd have to look through each one to see if you wanted to read it, and then you'd have to decide what to keep and what to discard. If you just went to your library instead whenever you wanted to find something to read, you could browse through the magazines there, look at interesting articles, and move on.

Usenet News

The original Internet news exchange network is called Usenet News, a free global message system created by two graduate students in 1979. Usenet consists of seven major news categories, with groups arranged under each one.

comp	computer-related groups, with discussion of hardware, software, computer science, and other computing subjects.
news	groups related to Usenet News, including information for new users, lists of new groups, and files of Frequently Asked Questions, or FAQs.
rec	groups about recreational interests and hobbies, including sports, music, television, and film.
sci	groups for professionals in the sciences.
soc	groups concerning social issues about different groups, cultures, or countries.
talk	groups for debating controversial issues.

misc   miscellaneous groups that don't fit neatly into any of the other six categories.

In addition to the basic six, there are many other widely circulated newsgroup categories. These others include categories such as **alt**, for alternative groups, and **k12**, a collection of newsgroups on subjects of interest to teachers and students from kindergarten through 12th grade. The alt category has a discussion group called **alt.kids-talk**, and **k12** includes similar groups called **k12.chat.elementary**, **k12.chat.junior**, and **k12.chat.senior**. As you can see, newsgroup names are set up like domain names, with parts separated by periods. The major difference is that newsgroup names start with the broadest category, such as **k12**, and become more specific as you move to the right. So the three groups just mentioned above are in the **k12** category, and the next part of their names, **.chat,** tells you that they are on-line meeting places for kids to talk. The last part of their names is the most specific, telling you what grade level each group serves, elementary, junior, or senior. There are thousands of newsgroups on Usenet, and more are added all the time. It's always a good idea to read a newsgroup for a while before sending out your own posts to the group. This helps you to get a sense of what the other regular posters are like and what topics are generally discussed.

Telnet

Telnet, also called remote login, lets you connect to a computer located somewhere else and work on it *interactively*. From your school or home computer, you can use telnet to get to other computers at schools, organizations, and companies worldwide and use them as if you were right there. Telnet is the protocol and software that makes this communication possible. Internet users talk about "telneting" to other sites, as in "Yesterday I telneted to the Library of Congress."

Window 1 (Configuration dialog)

Session name   hermes.merit.edu

Window Name

☐ FTP session (⌘F)

☐ Serial/SLIP (⌘S)

[Configure]   [OK]   [Cancel]

Window 2 (hermes.merit.edu 1 — Main Menu)

hermes.merit.edu 1

```
*    NOTE:---------> New users, please select option "H" on the main menu:    *
*                   H) Help and information for new users                     *
-------------------------------------------------------------------------------
Press Return for menu, or enter 3 letter forecast city code:

                    WEATHER UNDERGROUND MAIN MENU
                    *****************************
                  1) U.S. forecasts and climate data
                  2) Canadian forecasts
                  3) Current weather observations
                  4) Ski conditions
                  5) Long-range forecasts
                  6) Latest earthquake reports
                  7) Severe weather
                  8) Hurricane advisories
                  9) National Weather Summary
                 10) International data
                 11) Marine forecasts and observations
                 12) Ultraviolet light forecast
                 13) K-12 School Weather Observations
                 14) Weather summary for the past month
                  X) Exit program
                  C) Change scrolling to screen
                  H) Help and information for new users
                  ?) Answers to all your questions
                     Selection:█
```

Window 3 (hermes.merit.edu 1 — MichNet)

hermes.merit.edu 1

```
%Merit:Hermes (HME738:TN01:VT100:EDIT=MTS)
%You have reached MichNet, operated by Merit Network, I
%Enter a destination, or enter HELP for assistance.

Which Host?um-weather█
```

▲▶

With telnet, you can connect to remote computers, such as this weather server at the University of Michigan, and access their resources from your own computer. This telnet client is NCSA-Telnet for the Macintosh. As with most other TCP/IP-compliant Internet programs, it is available to students free over the Net at many software archives.

Window 4 (hermes.merit.edu 1 — Weather report)

hermes.merit.edu 1

```
Weather Conditions at 2 PM EDT on 12 JUL 95 for New York, NY.
Temp(F)    Humidity(%)    Wind(mph)    Pressure(in)    Weather
==============================================================
  79          68%         ESE at 8       30.10       Mostly Cloudy
BRONX-KINGS (BROOKLYN)-NASSAU-NEW YORK (MANHATTAN)-QUEENS-
RICHMOND (STATEN IS.)-
300 PM EDT WED JUL 12 1995

  TONIGHT...PARTLY CLOUDY AND MUGGY WITH FOG DEVELOPING. LOW IN THE
UPPER 60S. WIND LIGHT AND VARIABLE.
  THURSDAY...EARLY MORNING CLOUDS AND FOG THEN HAZY SUNSHINE. WARM AND
HUMID WITH HIGHS IN THE UPPER 80S...COOLER NEAR THE OCEAN. WIND SOUTH
AROUND 10 MPH.
  THURSDAY NIGHT...MOSTLY CLEAR AND MUGGY. LOW IN THE LOWER 70S.
  FRIDAY...HAZY HOT AND HUMID. HIGH 90 TO 95...COOLER NEAR THE OCEAN.

                    ********************
                     Storm damage report
                    ********************

093
WWUS30 KNYC 121859
LSRNYC

LOCAL STORM REPORT
NATIONAL WEATHER SERVICE NEW YORK NY
300 PM EDT WED JUL 12 1995

...SUMMARY OF STORM REPORTS FOR TUESDAY JULY 11 1995...


TIME    COUNTY       CITY         ST     EVENT

405 PM PUTNAM       KENT CLIFFS    NY     GOLF BALL SIZE HAIL
                                          COVERED STATE ROUTE 301

457 PM ORANGE       MAYBROOK       NY     PEA SIZE HAIL

625 PM NEW HAVEN    MERIDEN        CT     3/4 INCH HAIL

930 PM UNION        PLAINFIELD     NJ     1 TO 1 1/2 INCH HAIL

MCKILLOP



   Press Return to continue, M to return to menu, X to exit: █
```

You may wonder why you would want to connect to other computers. With telnet, you can use Internet resources that aren't available on your *local* machine. Many schools load information about projects that their students have developed onto their computer system. Hundreds of libraries around the world have put their catalogs on computer, so you can look up books from outside the library. And if you're away from home and have access to a computer connected to the Internet, you can use telnet to connect to your local E-mail account and check your mail. With telnet, you can instantly connect to sites on the other side of the globe and have access to databases and catalogs.

For example, the University of Michigan maintains a service called the Weather Underground that lets you access National Weather Service forecasts and weather conditions nationwide. This service is accessible from the University of Michigan's public network, called MichNet. To telnet to MichNet, you need to start your computer's telnet program, often referred to as the telnet *client*, and tell it to connect to MichNet's address, **hermes.merit.edu**, in the space where your telnet client asks for the host address or session name. This makes the connection between your computer and the one at MichNet.

After a few moments, MichNet's introductory screen appears. Telnet programs are actually a specialized type of terminal program, and like most terminal programs, they are character-based, so we see only letters, numbers, and symbols. Typing **um-weather** at the **Which host?** prompt brings you to the Weather Underground's introductory screen, and pressing return (or enter) again brings you to the Weather Underground's main menu. By navigating through the Weather Underground's various menus, you can obtain forecasts for any region of the United States and Canada.

File Transfer

Another popular Internet function is file transfer, or ftp, which stands for File Transfer Protocol. It is the standard set of rules that lets your computer bring back copies of files from other sites on the Internet, or in some cases, copy files from your computer to remote sites. Almost any kind of file that can be stored on a computer can be copied and brought back using ftp. *Text files* of stories, *picture files* and *sound files*, software programs, and instructional kits all can be copied with ftp. Schools, companies, and organizations all over the world have set aside space on their computers for *archives* of information that they'd like to share with the rest of the Internet community. Files from these archives can then be copied, or ftped, by users anywhere. It's like being able to browse through millions of file cabinets from your computer. These sites have agreed to let people log in to their computers using the user ID **anonymous**, so they are frequently called "anonymous ftp sites." Other ftp sites are not public. They require their users to have private accounts to access their archives.

Just as with telnet, you need to know the address of the computer you want to connect to before you begin. Let's say you want to connect to an anonymous ftp site at the University of Washington with the address **wuarchive.wustl.edu**. You type **wuarchive.wustl.edu** when your ftp client *prompts* you to enter

▶
**Using an ftp client such as this one by
Spry is one way of downloading files from
remote archives. Clicking with a mouse
on any of the directories shown at this
archive will cause the program to list the
contents of that directory.**

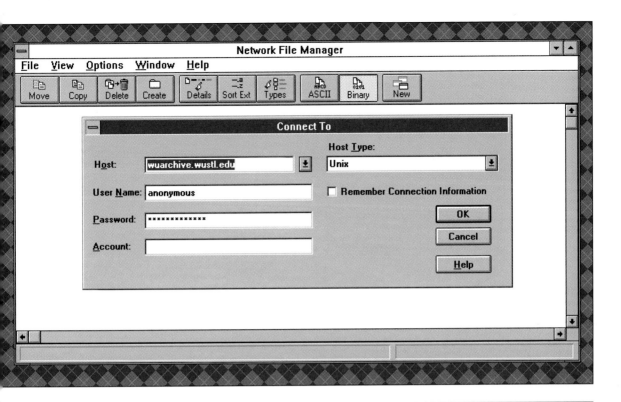

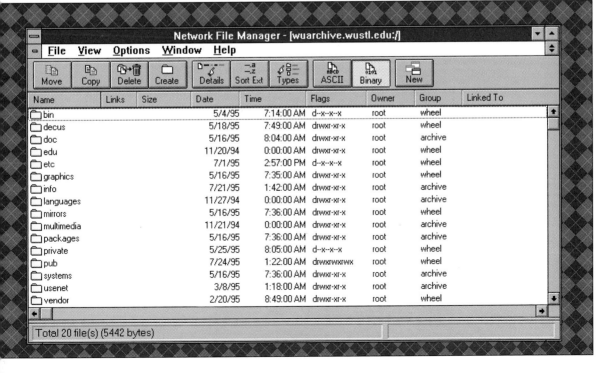

the address of the archive you wish to connect to. You will also be prompted to enter your user ID and *password*. When logging onto anonymous archives, enter **anonymous** for your username and your E-mail address for your password.

Connecting to this ftp site allows you to look at their lists of documents, software, and other information that you can copy. There are two major types of entries: files, which you can copy to your local computer (called downloading); and directories, which lead you to more choices. Directories are ranked one above the other, which means you have to move level by level through the listings.

But how do you know what files are out there on **wuarchive.wustl.edu**? You'll have to browse through the system to find out. To do this, you'll need to use three primary ftp functions: list directory, change directory, and get files. Different ftp clients have different ways of executing these functions, so you'll have to acquaint yourself with the program you use. The list directory function allows you to see the contents of a directory, so once you've logged in, you'll use it to see what's in the first-level, or *root*, directory. Many anonymous ftp sites show a pub *subdirectory* in their root directory. Pub stands for public, and lets you know that this directory contains files that are interesting to the general public. The pub directory is always a good place to start browsing at an ftp site. To get to there, you're going to have to use the change directory function to change from the root directory to the public directory. Most graphical ftp browsers allow you to change directories by clicking with a mouse on the desired directory.

After you have listed the files in the directory, you can use the get file function to copy any files to your local computer. Most graphical ftp programs execute this function automatically when you click with your mouse on the file you want.

CHAPTER

TITLE

Finding Things on the Internet:
Archie, Gopher, Veronica, World Wide Web

So far all the Internet activities have one thing in common: you have to know the Internet address of the site you want to reach. That's not a problem if you already have a list of Internet addresses for ftp or telnet sites. But what if you're just starting out and you don't know where to begin? What if you just want to browse? There are several easy-to-use tools that help you find things on the Internet: Archie, Veronica, gopher, and the World Wide Web.

Archie

When you want to see if anyone has a particular file that you can copy using ftp, you can use Archie to search all the ftp sites at once. The Archie system stores an index of files located at ftp sites all over the world. Archie is also a search mechanism that looks through these files and brings back lists of files that

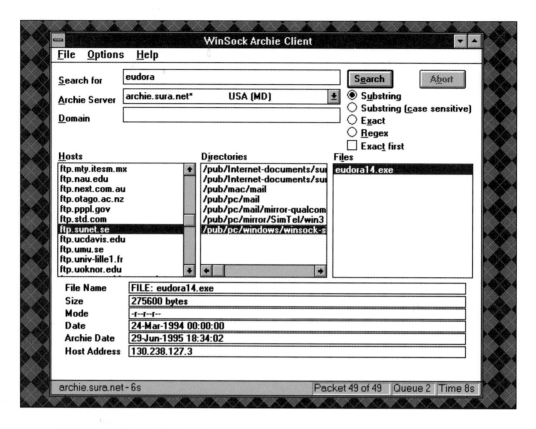

This Archie client for Windows will search for filenames containing the word or words entered in the "Search for" box. It also allows you to choose from an array of Archie servers in case some are not responsive. Here, the program lists file names containing the word **eudora** and the location of those files. This information can be used to download the file using ftp to your own machine.

match what you're looking for. The first version of Archie was created in 1989 by the staff of the McGill School of Computer Science in Quebec. When other universities showed interest in using this kind of finding tool, they wrote an Archie program for the public to use. The program is named Archie because it searches archive sites.

By 1992, the Archie database indexed more than fifteen hundred ftp sites. There are now more than twenty-one Archie servers running worldwide, all indexing the same number of ftp sites and updating their indexes monthly. You can use Archie by telneting to the nearest Archie server, or by using one of the many Archie clients available that automate the searches. Most Archie clients ask for a word or words contained in the names of the files you want to find. When Archie has finished your search, it shows you a list of ftp archives that have files containing the words in their names, and lists those filenames.

Gopher

Gopher is one of the easiest and most popular tools for finding information on the Internet. Gopher software helps solve the problem of locating Internet resources by arranging them in a series of menus. Instead of needing to know Internet addresses, you can use gopher to browse through lists of sites, and connect to them easily by selecting them from the menu. Gopher also brings together other tools such as ftp, telnet, and archie so that you can connect to other computers, search for files, and bring them back without ever leaving the gopher menu system. Gopher was developed in 1991 by a team of programmers at the University of Minnesota. Like Archie, gopher was designed to help meet the needs of a particular university; in this case, to deliver local information to the University of Minnesota community. This system was named the gopher because it is Minnesota's state animal and the University of Minnesota's mascot. Also, like errand runners who are asked to "go for" things, gopher programs run about the Internet for menus and files you've requested.

Gopher quickly became a useful tool for Internet users out-

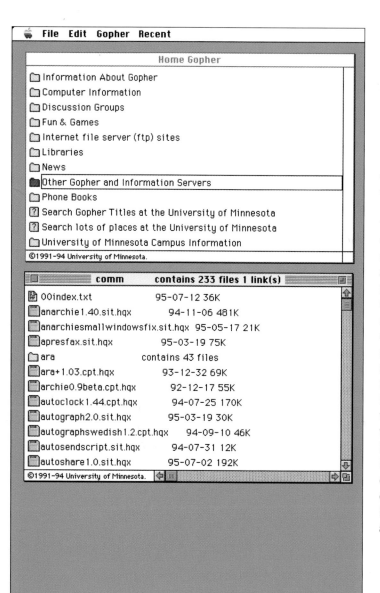

This gopher client for the Macintosh, Turbo Gopher, is a descendent of the original gopher program developed at the University of Minnesota. In this example, the top window lists entries at the University of Minnesota's home gopher, and the bottom window lists TCP/IP-compliant programs that can be downloaded by double clicking on them with a mouse. As with most gopher clients, Turbo Gopher tells you what kind of entries are displayed with the small icons to the left of the names. The folder icons indicate directories that lead to other menus. The question-mark icons indicate search mechanisms that will find entries with the word or words you enter. The document icons indicate text files. The disk icons indicate binary files that can be downloaded to your own computer. Some gopher clients include specific icons for picture and sound files as well.

side the university where it was developed. Thousands of schools, universities, businesses, and organizations have now developed their own gopher menus. These gophers usually give information about their home sites, but they also "point" to other sites around the globe. Gophers can point to ftp archive sites, telnet connections to other computers, Usenet newsgroups, Archie servers, phone directories, or other gophers. This brings the world of Internet resources together in a vast network of user-friendly menus.

Gophers are fun and easy to use. A gopher program may already be available to you on your local computer, or you can telnet to a public gopher site. There is a public gopher site located at the University of Michigan. To use this gopher, type **gopher.itd.umich.edu** in the space where your telnet client asks for the host address or session name.

The gopher menu generally uses a variety of symbols to tell you whether a menu item leads to a document, a software program, a picture, a phone book, a searchable database, or another menu. As with most Internet functions, the look of this menu will depend on your method of access.

Once you are connected to a gopher site such as the original gopher site at the University of Minnesota, you can move around by selecting menu items. From University of Minnesota's gopher, you can connect to other gophers, browse menus throughout *gopherspace*, and do things with the information you find. For instance, you can transfer files from other computers to your own machine. You may find sites that you want to check often that are buried deep in several layers of menus. Gopher lets you mark these sites with bookmarks, so you can return to them quickly without having to tunnel through the menus again. Like ftp archives, the menus are arranged in levels, so you get deeper into gopherspace as you follow the menus.

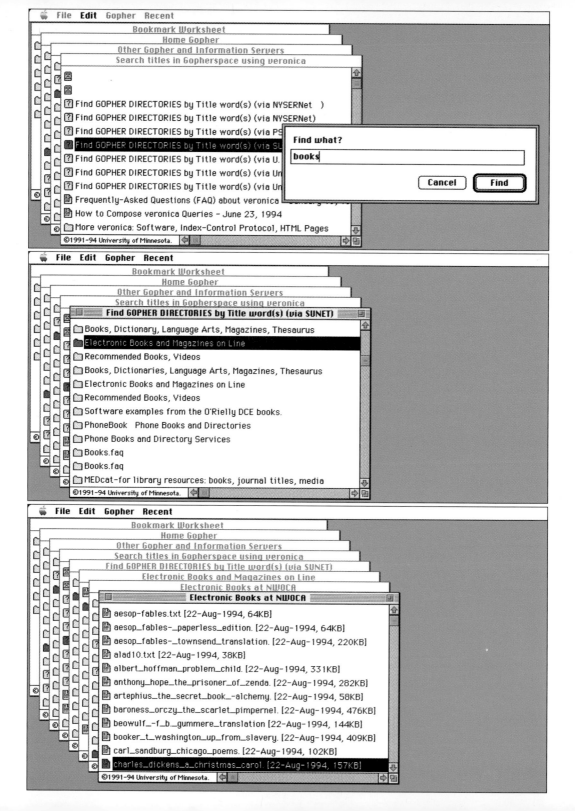

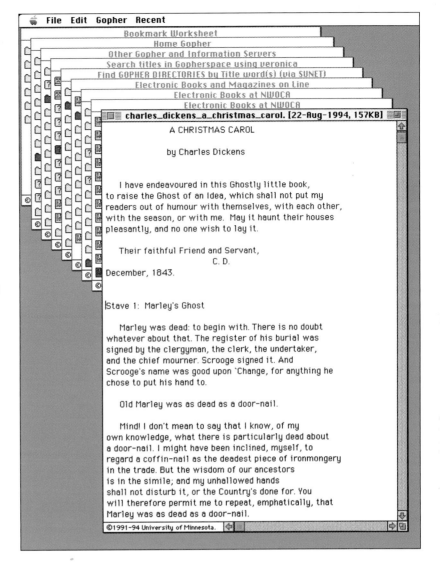

◄►
The University of Michigan's gopher site includes links to several Veronica servers. In this example, a search for entries containing the word **books** has led to a site offering electronic texts of many great literary works. Displayed in the last frame is the text of *A Christmas Carol* by Charles Dickens.

The text shown in the window reads:

File   Edit   Gopher   Recent

Bookmark Worksheet
Home Gopher
Other Gopher and Information Servers
Search titles in Gopherspace using veronica
Find GOPHER DIRECTORIES by Title word(s) (via SUNET)
Electronic Books and Magazines on Line
Electronic Books at NWOCA
Electronic Books at NWOCA

charles_dickens_a_christmas_carol. [22-Aug-1994, 157KB]

A CHRISTMAS CAROL

by Charles Dickens

I have endeavoured in this Ghostly little book,
to raise the Ghost of an Idea, which shall not put my
readers out of humour with themselves, with each other,
with the season, or with me. May it haunt their houses
pleasantly, and no one wish to lay it.

Their faithful Friend and Servant,
                                    C. D.

December, 1843.

Stave 1: Marley's Ghost

Marley was dead: to begin with. There is no doubt
whatever about that. The register of his burial was
signed by the clergyman, the clerk, the undertaker,
and the chief mourner. Scrooge signed it. And
Scrooge's name was good upon 'Change, for anything he
chose to put his hand to.

Old Marley was as dead as a door-nail.

Mind! I don't mean to say that I know, of my
own knowledge, what there is particularly dead about
a door-nail. I might have been inclined, myself, to
regard a coffin-nail as the deadest piece of ironmongery
in the trade. But the wisdom of our ancestors
is in the simile; and my unhallowed hands
shall not disturb it, or the Country's done for. You
will therefore permit me to repeat, emphatically, that
Marley was as dead as a door-nail.

©1991-94 University of Minnesota.

Veronica

Even though it's fun to browse through gopher menus, it's even more convenient to search all the menus at once for particular words. In 1992, a search tool for gopher menus was developed at the University of Nevada, Reno. This tool was named Veronica, or Very Easy Rodent-Oriented Net-wide Index to

Computerized Archives. This name is a joking reference to Archie, because Archie and Veronica are both characters in the same comic book. Veronica does for gopher menus what Archie does for ftp archive sites: it searches through them for the word or words you want to find and provides a list of the menu titles containing the words you've searched for. In January 1995, Veronica indexed 5,057 gophers, as well as information from about 5,000 other sources such as telnet sites. Veronica is actually a menu choice at many gopher sites. Like gopher and Archie, there are many public Veronica servers available.

World Wide Web

The newest and most exciting Internet navigation tool is the World Wide Web, called WWW or just the Web, for short. Researchers at CERN, the European Particle Physics Laboratory in Geneva, Switzerland, began developing the Web in 1990 as a way to help researchers share documents filled with charts and other graphic information that would be impossible to view with conventional Internet software. World Wide Web documents, or pages, are written in a language called hypertext. Hypertext pages contain highlighted words and images that lead directly to pictures, video clips, gophers, ftp archives, sound files, text, or software. These connections are called links, and you select them by clicking on them with a mouse. A hypertext document on the rain forest, for example, could have links to color images

▶

The Whole Internet Catalog, located at **http://www.gnn.com/wic/newrescat.toc.html,** is an excellent place to look for links to sites on all kinds of subjects. This page is displayed with Netscape for the Macintosh. Another excellent Internet directory is located at **http://www.yahoo.com.**

=== Netscape: The Whole Internet Catalog ===

| ⇦ Back | ⇨ Forward | 🏠 Home | 🔄 Reload | 🖼 Images | 📂 Open | 🖨 Print | 🔍 Find | ⊘ Stop | N

Location : http://www.gnn.com/wic/newrescat.toc.html

| What's New? | What's Cool? | Handbook | Net Search | Net Directory | Newsgroups |

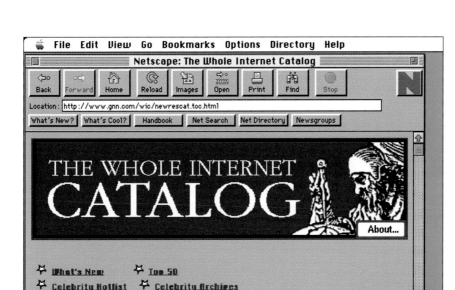

THE WHOLE INTERNET
CATALOG   About...

✦ **What's New**   ✦ **Top 50**
✦ **Celebrity Hotlist**   ✦ **Celebrity Archives**
✦ **All Subjects**   ✦ **All Catalog Entries**

The WIC is sponsored this week by MasterCard.

MasterCard International   **POINTERS**

Click here and you'll go places!

Arts & Entertainment

Architecture - Art Exhibits - Comics - Digital Images - E-Zines - Humor - Magazines - Movies - Music - Photography - Radio - Science Fiction - Sound Files - Television - Theater

Business & Finance

Agriculture - Career & Employment - Government Information - Internet Commerce - Investment - Management - Marketing - Nonprofits - Personal Finance - Real Estate - Small Business - Yellow Pages

Computers

Dictionaries - General Indexes - Graphics - Hardware Manufacturers - Languages & Programming - Macintosh - Magazines - Microsoft Windows - OS/2 - Publishing & Multimedia - Software & Shareware - Unix - Virtual Reality

Daily News

U.S. Newspapers - International Newspapers - Business News - Stock Quotes - Weather Report - Sports News - Daily Diversions

Document : Done.

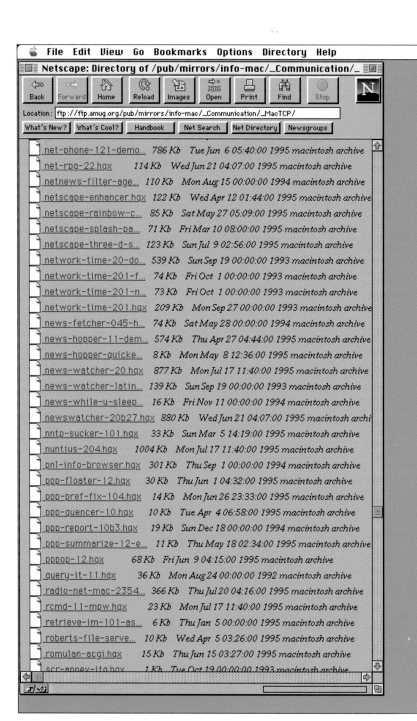

File   Edit   View   Go   Bookmarks   Options   Directory   Help

Netscape: Directory of /pub/mirrors/info-mac/_Communication/_

| Back | Forward | Home | Reload | Images | Open | Print | Find | Stop | N |

Location: ftp://ftp.amug.org/pub/mirrors/info-mac/_Communication/_MacTCP/

| What's New? | What's Cool? | Handbook | Net Search | Net Directory | Newsgroups |

net-phone-121-demo...   786 Kb   Tue Jun 6 05:40:00 1995 macintosh archive
net-rpg-22.hqx   114 Kb   Wed Jun 21 04:07:00 1995 macintosh archive
netnews-filter-age...   110 Kb   Mon Aug 15 00:00:00 1994 macintosh archive
netscape-enhancer.hqx 122 Kb   Wed Apr 12 01:44:00 1995 macintosh archive
netscape-rainbow-c...   85 Kb   Sat May 27 05:09:00 1995 macintosh archive
netscape-splash-pa...   71 Kb   Fri Mar 10 08:00:00 1995 macintosh archive
netscape-three-d-s... 123 Kb   Sun Jul 9 02:56:00 1995 macintosh archive
network-time-20-do...   539 Kb   Sun Sep 19 00:00:00 1993 macintosh archive
network-time-201-f...   74 Kb   Fri Oct 1 00:00:00 1993 macintosh archive
network-time-201-n...   73 Kb   Fri Oct 1 00:00:00 1993 macintosh archive
network-time-201.hqx   209 Kb   Mon Sep 27 00:00:00 1993 macintosh archive
news-fetcher-045-h...   74 Kb   Sat May 28 00:00:00 1994 macintosh archive
news-hopper-11-dem...   574 Kb   Thu Apr 27 04:44:00 1995 macintosh archive
news-hopper-quicke...   8 Kb   Mon May 8 12:36:00 1995 macintosh archive
news-watcher-20.hqx   877 Kb   Mon Jul 17 11:40:00 1995 macintosh archive
news-watcher-latin...   139 Kb   Sun Sep 19 00:00:00 1993 macintosh archive
news-while-u-sleep...   16 Kb   Fri Nov 11 00:00:00 1994 macintosh archive
newswatcher-20b27.hqx 880 Kb   Wed Jun 21 04:07:00 1995 macintosh archi
nntp-sucker-101.hqx   33 Kb   Sun Mar 5 14:19:00 1995 macintosh archive
nuntius-204.hqx   1004 Kb   Mon Jul 17 11:40:00 1995 macintosh archive
pnl-info-browser.hqx   301 Kb   Thu Sep 1 00:00:00 1994 macintosh archive
ppp-floater-12.hqx   30 Kb   Thu Jun 1 04:32:00 1995 macintosh archive
ppp-pref-fix-104.hqx   14 Kb   Mon Jun 26 23:33:00 1995 macintosh archive
ppp-quencer-10.hqx   10 Kb   Tue Apr 4 06:58:00 1995 macintosh archive
ppp-report-10b3.hqx   19 Kb   Sun Dec 18 00:00:00 1994 macintosh archive
ppp-summarize-12-e...   11 Kb   Thu May 18 02:34:00 1995 macintosh archive
pppop-12.hqx   68 Kb   Fri Jun 9 04:15:00 1995 macintosh archive
query-it-11.hqx   36 Kb   Mon Aug 24 00:00:00 1992 macintosh archive
radio-net-mac-2354...   366 Kb   Thu Jul 20 04:16:00 1995 macintosh archive
rcmd-11-mpw.hqx   23 Kb   Mon Jul 17 11:40:00 1995 macintosh archive
retrieve-im-101-as...   6 Kb   Thu Jan 5 00:00:00 1995 macintosh archive
roberts-file-serve...   10 Kb   Wed Apr 5 03:26:00 1995 macintosh archive
romulan-acgi.hqx   15 Kb   Thu Jun 15 03:27:00 1995 macintosh archive
scr-annex-ita.hqx   1 Kb   Tue Oct 19 00:00:00 1993 macintosh archive

of rain forests, to sound files of animal cries, and to gopher sites studying rain forests. Hypertext can bring together all kinds of media on the Internet in one document. The Web aims to let you use all the Internet resources available, no matter what type they are or where they are located, simply by selecting highlighted links.

Remember protocols? The Web uses three protocols: URL, HTML, and HTTP. Each Web page has an address, and these addresses are called Universal Resource Locators, or URLs. To reach a particular Web page, you must know its URL or find a link to that URL in another Web page. Hypertext Markup Language (HTML) is the formatting language that controls the layout of Web pages and provides tools for placing links in them. The last protocol, Hypertext Transfer Protocol (HTTP) controls the way hypertext documents are requested and sent over the network. World Wide Web browsers are also compatible with the other protocols we've seen, such as ftp and telnet. Here are some examples of how URLs can look:

> **ftp://wuarchive.wustl.edu/mirrors**
> **http://info.cern.ch:80/default.html**
> **telnet://dra.com**

The first part of the URL tells you what protocol the computer is going to use to get to the address. The first example uses ftp, the

◀

One of the reasons that the World Wide Web has become so popular is that it incorporates many different protocols and functions. Here, Netscape uses ftp to download News-Watcher, a news reader for the Macintosh, from a remote ftp archive. Notice that the address listed in the location box begins with ftp://.

🍎 **File Edit View Label Special**

Netscape: Welcome to Netscape

| ⇦ Back | ⇨ Forward | 🏠 Home | 🔄 Reload | 🖼 Images | ➡ Open | 🖨 Print | 🔍 Find | ⛔ Stop | N |

Netsite: http://home.netscape.com/

| What's New? | What's Cool? | Handbook | Net Search | Net Directory | Newsgroups |

WELCOME TO NETSCAPE

| ESCAPES | COMPANY & PRODUCTS | NETSCAPE STORE | NEWS & REFERENCE | ASSISTANCE | COMMUNITY |

✦ NETSCAPE SERVER GALLERIA ✦

SEC FILING
Netscape Communications Corporation files for initial public offering.

WINDOWS 95 NAVIGATOR BETA
Download the latest beta release of Netscape Navigator, specially tuned to take advantage of Win 95 interface enhancements and features.

SERVERMANIA THE WORLD OVER
Test drive a fully loaded Netscape Commerce or Communications Server for 60 days and win the race for business server solutions! Now enhanced for the enterprise - NT availability and improved access for users behind a firewall.

TEST DRIVE A NETSCAPE SERVER
60 DAYS. UNLIMITED MILEAGE.

WELCOME TO NETSCAPE!

ESCAPES	**NETSCAPE STORE**	**COMMUNITY**
What's New	Software	Netscape User Groups
What's Cool	Support	Internet White Pages
Net Directory	Publications	
Net Search		

COMPANY & PRODUCTS	**ASSISTANCE**	**NEWS & REFERENCE**
Netscape Products	About the Net	Internet Headlines
Netscape Sales	Support Programs	Netscape Press Releases
About Netscape	Creating Net Sites	Standards Docs
Partner Programs	Training Programs	Reference Material

Document: Done.

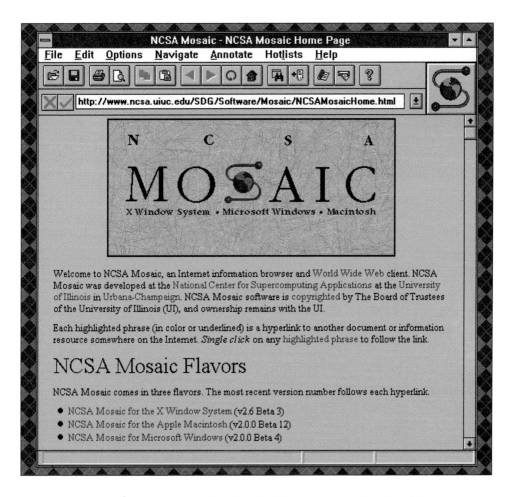

▲ Shown here is Mosaic's home page displayed on their own Web browser for Windows. NCSA has been a pioneer in developing Internet applications.

◄

From Netscape's home page at **http://home.netscape.com** you can download new versions of Netscape. This page also contains links to many other useful sites.

second uses HTTP, and the third uses telnet. Usually, a domain address follows the colon and double slashes (://). For example, the URL or Web address for CERN's information screen is **http://info.cern.ch**. The part of the URL to the right of the slashes, **info.cern.ch**, looks like the domain names we saw earlier.

The most flexible and exciting way to use the Web is with a graphical browser. There are many available, but the most popular graphical browsers are Mosaic and Netscape. The earliest graphical browser, NCSA Mosaic, was designed in 1993 at the National Center for Supercomputer Applications (NCSA) at the University of Illinois. By the end of that year, NCSA had released versions of Mosaic for the three most popular personal computer systems: Macintosh, Windows, and X Windows. This made the Web available to the general public, and usage soared. Graphical Web browsers can display documents with pictures, and highlight the links within documents with bright colors or icons. You use the mouse to place the cursor on a hypertext link, and activate the link by clicking. This takes you to another point on the Internet.

The number of Web sites is increasing dramatically. Thousands of schools, businesses, libraries, organizations, research centers, universities, and government agencies have created their own Web sites, called home pages. Because HTML is fairly easy to learn, individuals can write their own home pages, too.

CHAPTER

1 2 3 4

TITLE

Fun Places on the Internet

Now that you know what's on the Internet, and how to move around on it, you're ready to explore some of the thousands of fun sites out there. Every day, new information of interest to students is added to the Internet. Some is educational, some is recreational, and a lot of it is just plain fun! Gophers and Web sites offer some of the richest and fastest-growing collections of children's on-line resources. You can learn a new word every day by subscribing to a mailing list that sends you words and their definitions. You can read school newspapers and other students' project reports at Hillside Elementary School in Minnesota. You can look at greeting cards on-line that have been designed by people all over the world. Or you can visit museums and historical sites anywhere without leaving home. Some people have even set up Web pages that gather together hundreds of starting points for kids to explore. Here are just a few of the thousands of interesting places to visit on-line.

A.Word.A.Day

A.Word.A.Day is an on-line service that sends a new word, with its definition and pronunciation, to your E-mail account every morning. In addition to the word of the day, you will also get a daily quotation. To subscribe to A.Word.A.Day, you send an E-mail message to the address **wsmith@wordsmith.org**. In the subject line of your message you type **subscribe** followed by your first and last names. More than 7,500 people in 53 countries subscribe to A.Word.A.Day. There is also a Web page for A.Word.A.Day that can be reached at the URL address **http://lrdc5.lrdc.pitt.edu/awad/home.html**. From this home page, you can see the words for yesterday and today, subscribe to the service, look at the archives of words, or read the Frequently Asked Questions file about A.Word.A.Day.

Build-A-Card

A World Wide Web service called Build-A-Card appeared on Valentine's Day, 1995. The Build-A-Card Web page lets you look at over 2,000 greeting cards that people have created and sent on-line to their friends and family. You can build on their ideas to make your own card and actually put it on the Web for the world to see! This Web page has pictures you can use for a variety of occasions, such as birthday or holiday greetings. Choose images such as Star Trek characters or balloons and design your own message. The Build-A-Card Web page is located at **http://infopages.com/card/**.

Hillside Elementary School

One of the original school Web sites is maintained by Hillside Elementary School in Cottage Grove, Minnesota. In March, 1994, Hillside Elementary and the University of Minnesota College of Education announced its World Wide Web Page,

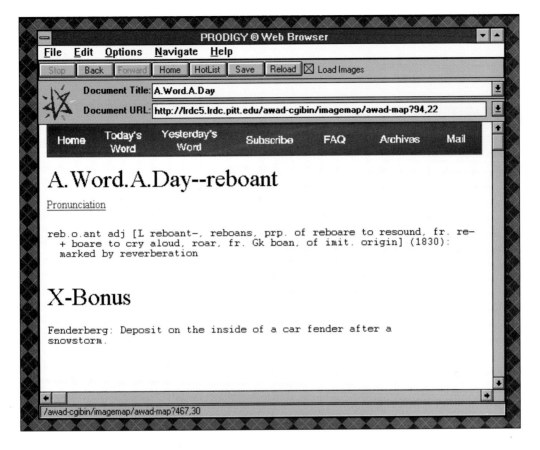

**This page from the A.Word.A.Day site is displayed
on Prodigy's Web browser for Windows.**

which showcases the ways students and teachers can use the
Internet. Students at Hillside worked with the Franklin Institute
Science Museum to create an interactive Web project. This pro-
ject, the Franklin Institute Workshop, helped students learn

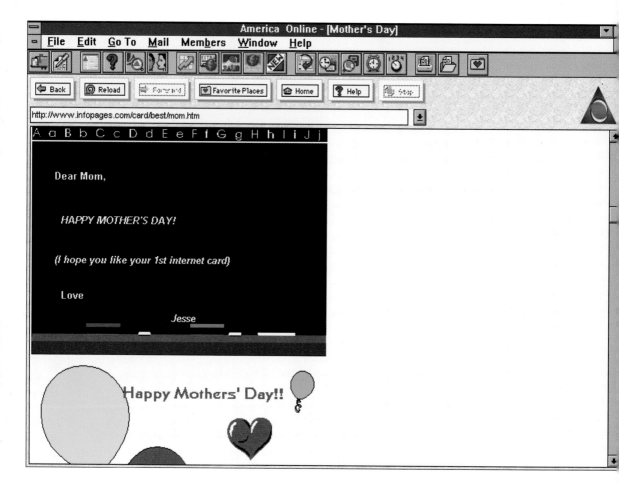

**This example of a card from the Build-A-Card site is
displayed on America Online's Web browser for Windows.**

World Wide Web skills like making documents using hypertext
markup language, loading graphic image files, and setting up
their own Web site. This site includes a link to the Franklin
Institute, which can connect to on-line educational exhibits on

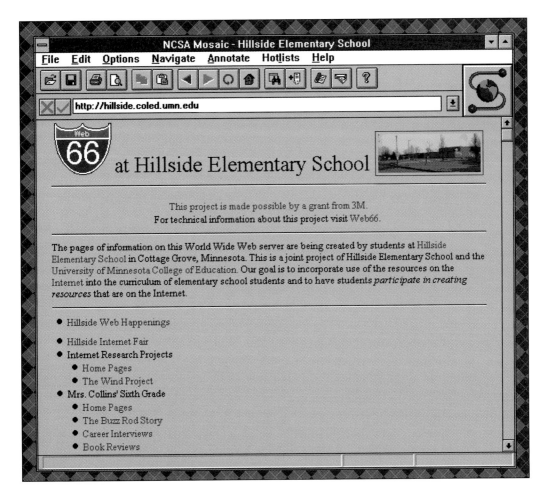

Shown here is Hillside Elementary School's home page displayed with Mosaic for Windows.

dinosaurs, astronomy, and mapmaking. Hillside's students have also put their school newspaper on the Web. One sixth-grade class at Hillside interviewed people in different jobs to find out what it was like to work as a chef, pilot, veterinarian, or pharmacist, and then loaded the career reports they'd written on to their home page. Hillside's Web site has been featured on the television program "Newton's Apple," and is mentioned in John December's book *The World Wide Web Unleashed*. You might get some ideas from this Web page for projects for your school. Hillside Elementary's URL is **http://hillside.coled.umn.edu**.

Virtual Exhibits

The World Wide Web can bring many on-line exhibitions on subjects like art, natural history, archaeology, and architecture right to your computer screen. Increasing numbers of museums are using scanners to capture color images of their exhibits, including photographs, objects, and maps. For example, portions of the Library of Congress exhibit on the Dead Sea Scrolls are available on-line at the following URL: **http://sunsite.unc.edu/expo/deadsea.scrolls.exhibit/intro.html**. This site shows images of 31 objects loaned by the Israel Antiquities Authority, including fragments of the Dead Sea Scrolls, artifacts from the excavation, and illustrations from the Library of Congress' collections.

The URL **http://155.187.10.12/fun/exhibits.html** takes you to a home page developed at the Australian National Botanic Gardens. This site features links to the Smithsonian Institution, Grand Canyon National Park, and the WWW Virtual Museums page, which includes exhibits by the Louvre in France and the Vatican in Italy.

►
Pictured here is the introduction to a Virtual Exhibit on the Dead Sea Scrolls. The Web browser is Netscape for the Macintosh.

Netscape: Dead Sea -- Intro

Back Forward Home Reload Images Open Print Find Stop N

Location : http://sunsite.unc.edu/expo/deadsea.scrolls.exhibit/intro.html

What's New? What's Cool? Handbook Net Search Net Directory Newsgroups

Welcome to

SCROLLS FROM THE DEAD SEA

The Ancient Library of Qumran and Modern Scholarship

an Exhibit at the Library of Congress, Washington, D C

The exhibition **Scrolls From the Dead Sea: The Ancient Library of Qumran and Modern Scholarship** brings before the American people a selection from the scrolls which have been the subject of intense public interest. Over the years questions have been raised about the scrolls' authenticity, about the people who hid them away, about the period in which they lived, about the secrets the scrolls reveal, and about the intentions of the scrolls' custodians in restricting access. The Library's exhibition describes the historical context of the scrolls and the Qumran community from whence they may have originated; it also relates the story of their discovery 2,000 years later. In addition, the exhibition encourages a better understanding of the challenge s and complexities connected with scroll research.

The exhibition is divided into five sections:

- Introduction -- The World of the Scrolls
- The Qumran Library
- The Qumran Community
- Today -- 2,000 Years Later
- Conclusion

The original exhibition included nearly 100 objects: scroll fragments, artifacts from the Qumran site, and books and illustrations from the Library of Congress' collections. The online exhibit includes images of 12 scroll fragments and 29 other objects lo aned by the Israel Antiquities Authority for this exhibition.

You may view the exhibit by selecting any of the above sections or you may choose to browse the entire exhibit by selecting

- Outline of Objects and Topics in **Scrolls from the Dead Sea**

More information about the exhibit can be found in

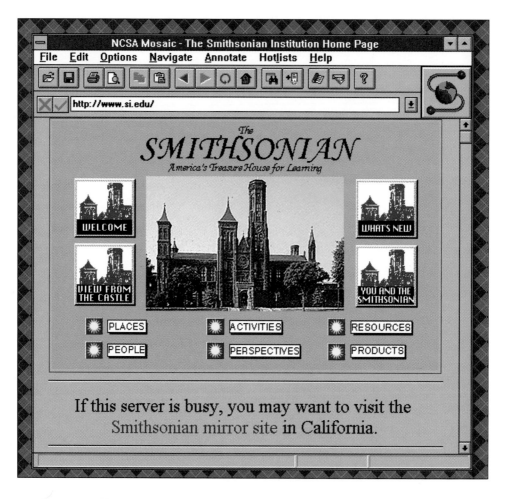

The Virtual Museums page contains a link to the Smithsonian Institution. The Smithsonian's welcome page is displayed here with Mosaic for Windows.

KIDLINK

KIDLINK is one of the oldest children's Internet sites around. Founded in 1990, KIDLINK is an organization dedicated to get-

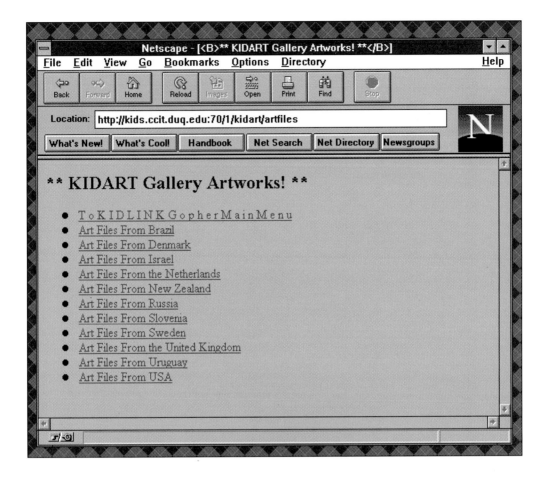

Netscape - [<B> KIDART Gallery Artworks! **</B>]**

File   Edit   View   Go   Bookmarks   Options   Directory   Help

Back   Forward   Home   Reload   Images   Open   Print   Find   Stop

Location: http://kids.ccit.duq.edu:70/1/kidart/artfiles

What's New!   What's Cool!   Handbook   Net Search   Net Directory   Newsgroups

** KIDART Gallery Artworks! **

- To K I D L I N K G o p h e r M a i n M e n u
- Art Files From Brazil
- Art Files From Denmark
- Art Files From Israel
- Art Files From the Netherlands
- Art Files From New Zealand
- Art Files From Russia
- Art Files From Slovenia
- Art Files From Sweden
- Art Files From the United Kingdom
- Art Files From Uruguay
- Art Files From USA

**The KIDLINK site offers examples of artwork by kids all over
the world. This menu is shown on Netscape for Windows.**

ting as many children ages 10 to15 as possible involved in a
global exchange with each other. Since it started, over 30,000
children from 67 countries have participated in KIDLINK.
Children tell each other about themselves and exchange their
views on the future of our world. All children have to do to par-

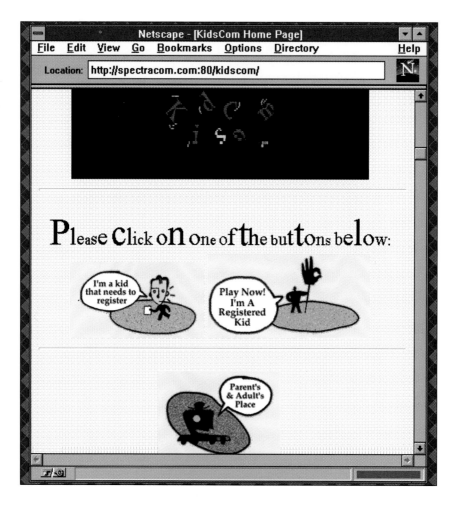

**This KidsCom home page is
displayed with Netscape for Windows.**

ticipate in KIDLINK is answer the following four questions: 1)
Who am I? 2) What do I want to be when I grow up? 3) How do
I want the world to be better when I grow up? and 4) What can

I do now to make this happen? There are several ways to get to KIDLINK. Its gopher address is **kids.duq.edu**, and its Web page with the same information can be reached at the following URL: **http://kidlink.ccit.duq.edu**.

KIDLINK registration forms can be found on their gopher and Web sites, or you can register by E-mailing answers to the four questions to **response@vm1.nodak.edu**. Once you have registered, you are welcome to enjoy all the KIDLINK services available. Some of the many ways KIDLINK connects kids worldwide include their newsletter, which can be read on-line or subscribed to, and their discussion forums. KIDCAFE is a round-the-clock conferencing system where children 10 to 15 can talk about any topic, make friends, and share interests in any language. There are additional lists for discussion in Japanese, Portuguese, Spanish, and Scandinavian languages.

KidsCom

Another fun Web site is KidsCom. It can be reached at the URL **http://www.spectracom.com/kidscom**. KidsCom is an on-line communications playground for children between the ages of 8 and 12. Once you register, KidsCom can set you up with an on-line pen pal, called a Key Pal, take you to a geography game, or let you write virtual grafitti on the Web. The KidsCom Web page includes a link to the registration form called Who Do Ya Wanna Be? This form asks you about yourself, your family, your interests, and your future. Once you complete and send the registration form, you're free to wander through the KidsCom services to find a Key Pal, ask questions, or play with the Virtual Grafitti wall.

Fun Page

The sites above were created by people at organizations, schools, or companies. With the increase in World Wide Web

Netscape: Fun & games

Back   Forward   Home   Reload   Images   Open   Print   Find   Stop   N

Location: http://condor.bcm.tmc.edu/fun.html

What's New?   What's Cool?   Handbook   Net Search   Net Directory   Newsgroups

Taking a break from biology....

last updated 5/22/95

**If you find something you like on this fun page, a[d]
may not stay here forever.**

This list contains links to zoom you down to the appropriate pa[ge]

- stuff for kids and for parents
- literature and publications
- maps, weather, and travel
- museum exhibits & art
- universities and other academic links
- games and hobbies
- a little bit of science that's not biology
- job search information
- sports
- commercial services
- local (Houston or Texas) stuff
- general network stuff
- financial stuff
- new stuff
- miscellaneous

stuff for kids and for parents

kids (*also see games and hobbies, below*)

toys and simple games

- Mr. Potato Head
- Blue Dog can count!
- Carlos' Coloring Book Home
- WWW Spirograph
- Lite-Brite pictures
- TicTacToe from BU's games page

collections of links for kids

- Kids on the Web
- Stephen Savitzky's Interesting places for kids on the W[eb]
- Italian Children's Page; The Canadian Kids Home Pag[e]
- Latitude28 Schoolhouse
- KID list
- Kids Web "A World Wide Web Digital Library for S[tudents]
- The Web as a Learning Tool
- CyberKids Launchpad
- Berit's Best Sites for Children (from Theodore Tugbo[at]

Netscape: Cyberkids #3 Cover

Back   Forward   Home   Reload   Images   Open   Print   Find   Stop

Location: http://www.mtlake.com/cyberkids/Issue3/Issue3Cover.html

What's New?   What's Cool?   Handbook   Net Search   Net Directory   Newsgroups

Issue #3, July-September 1995

- More stories from Mountain Lake Software's 1994 Story Contest

- Young immigrants tell their stories of coming to America

- Product review: Crossword Companion

- Game: Whose Flag Is It?

View the Table of Contents.

Go to CyberKids Home Page.

access, more and more individuals are designing their own Web pages of interesting or amusing links to other pages, and making them public. Paula Burch of Baylor College of Medicine in Houston has developed a huge and wonderful Web site called Fun Page, which brings together links to hundreds of other sites of interest to kids, parents, and teachers. Just a few of the great things you'll find on Fun Page are links to sites on children's stories and poems, nature photographs, games and hobbies, science, and sports. Fun Page can be reached at the URL **http://condor.bcm.tmc.edu/fun.html**.

These are just some starting points for your Internet exploration. After you're familiar enough with the Web, you may want to design your own personal home page!

◀

Fun Page contains links to many interesting sites such as this on-line magazine for kids. Both the Fun Page menu and the CyberKids page are displayed with Netscape for the Macintosh.

Glossary

account permission to use a computer on a network (such as the Internet) including certain resources, such as hard-disk space. An account is generally accessed with a user ID and a password.

archive a collection of information in the form of computer files that is stored on a computer on the Internet for users to read and copy.

client a program dedicated to performing a specific Internet function, such as E-mail or ftp.

download to copy a file from a remote computer to a local computer.

gopherspace the sum of all sites on the Internet that can be accessed with a gopher program.

host a computer that provides services to users over a network.

interactive allowing two-way communication between computers.

local at a location the same as your own. It is generally used to refer to the computer you are working on or information and services that originate from that computer.

modem a computer peripheral that allows computer data to be transmitted over telephone lines.

network two or more computers connected together for communication.

password an identifying series of letters and/or numbers used with a user ID to log into an account.

picture file a computer file consisting of a digitized picture that can be displayed on a computer screen. These files usually end with the code .jpg or .gif. Such codes are called extensions.

post a note sent to a Usenet newsgroup or an Internet mailing list. The note is accessible by all other subscribers to a group or list.

prompt to ask for some kind of response or action.

remote at a location different from your own. It is generally used to describe distant computers or information and services that originate from a distant computer and travel over a network to the computer you are working on.

root the original level of a disk or archive. All other directories are subdirectories of the root directory.

server a computer that provides a service to other computers on a network. Frequently, a server is dedicated to a specific function, such as processing E-mail.

site a location of information on the Internet. Sites are usually representative of a person or organization.

sound file a computer file consisting of a digitized sound that can be played through a properly equipped computer. These files usually end with the code .snd, .au, or .wav. Such codes are called extensions.

standard an agreed-upon set of procedures.

subdirectory a directory that is located within another directory. All directories other than the root are subdirectories of some other directory.

text file a computer file consisting of letters, numbers, and assorted symbols. These files usually end with the code .txt or .doc. Such codes are called extensions.

user ID an abbreviation for *user identification*. It is a unique, personal series of letters (often an abbreviation of a person's name) and/or numbers that, with a password, identifies an account.

workstation a properly equipped computer and its peripherals.

Index

Macintosh, *22–23, 24–25, 36, 40–41*, 46, *52–53, 58–59*
Mailing lists, 22–24
Mail servers, 16
Microsoft Windows, *22–23, 34, 45*, 46, *49, 50, 51, 54, 55, 56*
Modem, 16, 20
Mosaic Web browser for Windows, *45*, 46, *51, 54*

National Center For Supercomputer Applications (NCSA), *45*, 46
Netscape, *14*, 17, *42–43 44–45*
Netscape for Macintosh, 40–41, 46, *52–53, 58–59*
Netscape for Windows, *55, 56*
Newsgroup categories, 26–27
Newsgroups, 22, 24–27, 37
News-Watcher for the Macintosh, *24–25, 43*
Non-standard protocols, 20

Packet switchers. *See* routers
Passwords, 30
Phone lines, 11, 16, 20
Pipeline, the, 20
Point to Point Protocol (PPP), *18*, 20
Posts, 24
Prodigy, *18*, 20
Prodigy's Web browser for Windows, *49*
Pub directory, 32

Remote computers, 16, 17, *28*
Remote login. *See* Telnet

Root directory, 32
Routers, 11

Serial Line Internet Protocol (SLIP), *18*, 20
Spry ftp client, *30–31*
Spry newsreader. *See* Air News for the PC

Telnet, 27–29, *28*, 30, 35, 37, 43, 46
Telnet sites, 33
Transmission Control Protocol (TCP), 11, 16, 20, *28, 36*
Turbo Gopher, *36*

Universal Resource Locators (URL), 43, 46, 48, 52, 57, 59
Usenet News, 26, 37
User ID, 13, 20, 30
User name. *See* User ID

Veronica (Very Easy Rodent-Oriented Net-wide Index to Computerized Archives), 33, *38–39, 39–40*
Virtual exhibits, 52–54, *52–53, 54*

Weather Underground, 29
Web, the. *See* World Wide Web
Whole Internet Catalog, *40–41*
World Wide Web (WWW), *14–15*, 17, 20, 33, 40–46, 48–49
World Wide Web sites, 47, 48, 52, 57, 59
World Wide Web Unleashed, The (December), 52

X Windows, 46

About the Author

Kerry Cochrane is the Head of Reference at Cudahy Library at Loyola University of Chicago. She has previously been adjunct faculty at Rosary College in Chicago teaching Online Searching and the Internet. She holds a master's degree in library science and a bachelor of art's degree in English, both from the University of Iowa.